U0131497

冰與火之歌之
小惡魔的大智慧

The Wit & Wisdom of Tyrion Lannister

George R. R. Martin
喬治·馬汀

整理 林零

高寶書版集團

On Being a Dwarf

論身為侏儒

All dwarfs are bastards in their father's eyes.

——A Game of Thrones

全天下的侏儒，在父親的眼裡與私生子無異。

——《權力遊戲》上冊 p.87

What joy to be a dwarf.

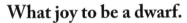

——*A Dance with Dragons*

身為侏儒還有這種好處。

——《與龍共舞》中冊 p.404

I was born. I lived. I am guilty of being a dwarf, I confess it. And no matter how many times my good father forgave me, I have persisted in my infamy.

——*A Storm of Swords*

我出生，然後活下來，因身為侏儒而有罪。這點我認罪，無論我的好父親原諒多少次，我還是惡名昭彰。

——《劍刃風暴》下冊 p.240

Whatever you wear, you're still a dwarf. You'll never be as tall as that knight on the steps, him with his long straight legs and hard stomach and wide manly shoulders.

——*A Storm of Swords*

不管穿什麼，你仍舊是個侏儒。你永遠也不可能像階梯上的那名高大的騎士，有他修長而筆直的腿、堅硬的腹肌及寬闊、充滿男子氣概的肩膀。

——《劍刃風暴》上冊 p.222

I have been called many things, but giant is seldom one of them.

——*A Game of Thornes*

我有過的綽號不少，不過「巨人」還是第一次聽到。

——《權力遊戲》上冊 p.284

The only thing more pitiful than a dwarf without a nose is a dwarf without a nose who has no gold.

——*A Dance with Dragons*

比起缺了鼻子的侏儒，更慘的是什麼呢？就是缺了鼻子又沒錢的侏儒啊！

——《與龍共舞》上冊 p.35

Pissing is the least of my talents. You ought to see me shit.

——A Dance with Dragons

撒尿是我最不出色的長處，你們應該看我拉屎才對。

——《與龍共舞》上冊 p.158

No one fears a dwarf.

——A Dance with Dragons

沒有人會怕侏儒。

——《與龍共舞》上冊 p.39

All dwarfs may be bastards, yet not all bastards need be dwarfs.

——A Game of Thornes

全天下的侏儒都可能被視為私生子，私生子卻未必被人當成侏儒。

——《權力遊戲》上冊 p.87

I'm short, not blind.

——*A Clash of Kings*

我個子雖矮，但眼睛沒瞎。

——《烽火危城》上冊 p.85

Do you think I might stand taller in black?

——A Dance with Dragons

妳覺得若是我穿了一身黑，會不會顯得高一些？

——《與龍共舞》上冊 p.37

I am malformed, scarred, and small, but…abed, when the candles are blown out, I am made no worse than other men. In the dark, I am the Knight of Flowers.

——*A Storm of Swords*

我是畸形難看、臉上到處有疤且個頭矮小，不過……當蠟燭吹熄後，我在床上的表現並不比任何男人差。黑暗中，我就是百花騎士。

——《劍刃風暴》中冊 p.36

Dwarfs are a jape of the gods, but men make eunuchs.

——A Clash of Kings

侏儒雖是諸神的惡作劇⋯⋯可太監卻是人為的產物。

——《烽火危城》上冊 p.159

They say I'm half a man. What dose that make the lot of you?

——*A Clash of Kings*

人家都說我是「半人」，那你們這些人又算什麼？

——《烽火危城》下冊 p.378

I have a tender spot in my heart for cripples and bastards and broken things.

———*A Game of Thornes*

我特別同情殘廢、私生子和其他畸形怪胎。

———《權力遊戲》上冊 p.333

The gods must have been drunk when they got to me.

——*A Dance with Dragons*

神一定是喝醉了，才把我做成這副德性。

——《與龍共舞》上冊 p.253

I only need half my wits to be a match for you.

——*A Dance with Dragons*

一招半式就夠收拾你了。

——《與龍共舞》上冊 p.264

I had dreamt enough for one small life. And of such follies: love, justice, friendship, glory. As well dream of being tall.

——A Dance with Dragons

短短的人生中已經做了夠多的夢，愚蠢的諸如愛情、正義、友誼與榮耀。乾脆夢一下自己長高如何。

——《與龍共舞》上冊 p.29

It may be good luck to rub the head of a dwarf, but it is even better luck to suck on a dwarf's cock.

——*A Dance with Dragons*

摸侏儒的頭，會帶來好運。而吸一下侏儒的下面，運氣會更好喔。

——《與龍共舞》上冊 p.396

On the Power of Words

論言語之力量

My mind is my weapon. My brother has his
sword, King Robert has his warhammer, and I
have my mind…and a mind needs books as a
sword needs a whetstone if it is to keep its edge.

——A Game of Thornes

我的頭腦就是我的武器！老哥有他的寶劍，勞勃國王有他
的戰鎚，我則有我的腦袋瓜。人若想保持思路清晰銳利，
就得多讀書，猶如寶劍需要磨刀石一樣。

——《權力遊戲》上冊 p.175

Duck has his sword, I my quill and parchment.

——*A Dance with Dragons*

鴨子會使劍，我會動筆啊。

——《與龍共舞》上冊 p.259

When you tear out a man's tongue, you are not proving him a liar, you're only telling the world that you fear what he might say.

——*A Clash of Kings*

拔了一個人的舌頭，無法證明他是騙子，反倒是讓全世界知道，你有多怕他說出來的話。

——《烽火危城》上冊 p.262

Sleep is good. And books are better.

——*A Clash of Kings*

睡覺很好，讀書更好。

——《烽火危城》上冊 p.509

Let them see that their words can cut you, and you'll never be free of the mockery. If they want to give you a name, take it, make it your own. Then they can't hurt you with it anymore.

——*A Game of Thrones*

一旦別人發現了綽號對你的殺傷力，這綽號就跟定你啦。既然他們愛幫你取綽號，就大大方方接受，最好還裝出樂在其中的樣子，那他們就再也傷不了你。

——《權力遊戲》上冊 p.256

Guard your tongue before it digs your grave.

——*A Storm of Swords*

管好自己的舌頭前，你在自掘墳墓。

——《劍刃風暴》下冊 p.168

Words are wind.

——*A Dance with Dragons*

話語如風。

——《與龍共舞》上冊 p.416

On Romance

論愛情

Shy maids are my favorite sort. Aside from wanton ones...but sometimes the ugliest ones are the hungriest once abed.

——*A Dance with Dragons*

醜胚的女孩我可是愛得很，當然豪放女也不錯……但往往醜女上了床後，反而熱情如火。

——《與龍共舞》上冊 p.162、168

My own father could not love me. Why would you if not for gold?

——*A Dance with Dragons*

連親生父親都不愛我，妳若不是為了錢怎麼可能會理我？

——《與龍共舞》上冊 p.331

A man grows weary of having no lovers but his fingers.

——*A Dance with Dragons*

沒情人，只有手指，也是會膩的呀。

——《與龍共舞》上冊 p.403

I plant my little seeds just as often as I can.

——*A Storm of Swords*

我可是很努力地四處散播我的小種子。

——《劍刃風暴》上冊 p.356

With whores, the young ones smell much better, but the old ones know more tricks.

——*A Dance with Dragons*

至少就妓女這一行，年輕的雖然比較漂亮，但年紀大的懂得技巧更多喔！

——《與龍共舞》中冊 p.31

I would prefer a whore who is reasonably young, with as pretty a face as you can find. If she has washed sometimes this year, I shall be glad. If she wasn't, wash her.

——*A Game of Thornes*

最好是年輕一點的，當然，愈漂亮愈好。如果她今年洗過澡，那最好；如果沒有，把她洗乾淨吧！

——《權力遊戲》下冊 p.344

Sleep with Lollys? I'd sooner cut it off and feed it to the goats.

——A Storm of Swords

跟洛麗絲上床？我寧可砍掉自己的老二去餵山羊。

——《劍刃風暴》上冊 p.355

**Your Grace, if you take my tongue, you will leave
me no way at all to pleasure this sweet wife you
gave me.**

——*A Storm of Swords*

如果您割了我的舌頭，我可就無法享用您賜給我的美麗新
娘。

——《劍刃風暴》中冊 p.33

A dwarf's cock has magical powers.

　　　　　　　　　　——*A Dance with Dragons*

據說侏儒的寶貝有魔力喔。

　　　　　　　　　——《與龍共舞》上冊 p.386

On Family Values

論家庭價值

A Lannister always pays his debts.

——A Game of Thrones

蘭尼斯特家人有債必償。

——《權力遊戲》上冊 p.439

I never bet against my family.

——A Game of Thrones

我只會把賭注下在自家人身上。

——《權力遊戲》上冊 p.450

Hard hands and no sense of humor makes for a bad marriage.

——A Dance with Dragons

出手不知輕重，加上缺乏幽默感，可不是什麼好的組合。

——《與龍共舞》中冊 p.32

I should say something, but what? Pardon me, Father, but it's our brother she wants to marry.

——*A Storm of Swords*

我應該說幾句話，不過要說什麼呢？不好意思，老爸，但她想嫁的是她弟弟，也就是我的老哥？

——《劍刃風暴》上冊 p.352

My sister has mistaken me for a mushroom. She keeps me in the dark and feeds me shit.

——*A Storm of Swords*

我老姊把我和一朵蘑菇搞混了。她把我關在暗無天日的地方，餵我吃狗屎。

——《劍刃風暴》上冊 p.80

Kinslaying is dry work. It gives a man a thirst.

——*A Dance with Dragons*

連自己的親爹都可以殺，那喝酒不過小事一樁。

——《與龍共舞》上冊 p.43

Have no fever, I won't kill you, you are no kin of mine.

——A Dance with Dragons

別擔心，我不會殺你，反正你又不是我親戚。

——《與龍共舞》上冊 p.170

The man who kills his own blood is cursed forever in the sight of gods and men.

——*A Clash of Kings*

殺害血親將招致人神共憤。

——《烽火危城》下冊 p.169

I learned long ago that it is considered rude to vomit on your brother.

——*A Game of Thrones*

很久以前我就學到教訓：在你哥哥身上嘔吐，是很不禮貌的事。

——《權力遊戲》上冊 p.85

Kinslaying was not enough, I needed a cunt and wine to seal my ruin.

——*A Dance with Dragons*

殺了自己父親還不夠，要有女人和酒，才可以保證我走上末路。

——《與龍共舞》下冊 p.125

I have never liked you, Cersei, but you were my own sister, so I never did you harm. You've ended that. I will hurt you for this. I don't know how yet, but give me time. A day will come when you think you are safe and happy, and suddenly your joy will turn to ashes in your mouth, and you'll know the debt is paid.

——*A Clash of Kings*

我從來就沒喜歡過妳，瑟曦，但妳終究是我的親姊姊，所以我不曾傷害妳。不過從今天起，就不是這樣了。我會報復的，只是還不知用什麼方式。妳等著吧！將來會有那麼一天，當自以為平安快樂時，妳的喜樂會瞬間在口中化為灰燼，屆時就知道債還清了。

——《烽火危城》下冊 p.314

On the Human Condition

論人生處境

The gods are blind. And men see only what they wish.

——*A Dance with Dragons*

天神們根本就眼盲。至於人嘛，只看得見自己想看見的東西。

——《與龍共舞》中冊 p.30

Why is it that when one man builds a wall, the next man immediately needs to know what's on the other side?

——*A Game of Thrones*

為何世事總如此？有人蓋了牆，別人馬上就想知道牆的另一頭有什麼。

——《權力遊戲》上冊 p.255

I think life is a jape. Yours, mine, everyon's.

——A Dance with Dragons

反正人生不過如此，你、我、任何人都一樣，全是爛命一條。

——《與龍共舞》中冊 p.30

There has never been a slave who did not choose to be a slave. Their choice may be between bondage and death, but the choice is always there.

——*A Dance with Dragons*

淪為奴隸的人其實都是自己選的，不當奴隸或許會死，但真相卻是有做奴隸以外的選擇存在。

——《與龍共舞》下冊 p.277

Death is so terribly final, while life is full of possibilities.

——A Game of Thrones

死了就什麼都沒了，活著卻有無限可能。

——《權力遊戲》上冊 p.134

An honest kiss, a little kindness, everyone deserves that much, however big or small.

——*A Dance with Dragons*

真誠的吻、仁慈的對待，其實每個人理當都該得到，與身體的大小毫無關係。

——《與龍共舞》中冊 p.284

Every fool loves to hear that he's important.

——*A Dance with Dragons*

愚昧的人總感覺自己很重要。

——《與龍共舞》中冊 p.150

Never forget who you are, for surely the world will not. Make it your strength. Then it can never be your weakness. Armor yourself in it, and it will never be used to hurt you.

——*A Game of Thrones*

永遠不要忘記你是什麼人，因為別人不會忘。但要化阻力為助力，如此一來你就沒有弱點。用它來武裝自己，就沒有人可以用它來傷害你。

——《權力遊戲》上冊 p.87

**A little honest loathing might be refreshing like
a tart wine after too much sweet.**

——*A Dance with Dragons*

直接給我臉色，偶一為之還算新鮮，類似甜點吃多了要喝
杯酸酒。

——《與龍共舞》上冊 p.39

We all need to be mocked from time to time, lest we start to take ourselves too seriously.

——*A Game of Thrones*

我們不時需要被嘲弄，以免生活太過嚴肅。

——《權力遊戲》上冊 p.283

Men are such faithless creatures.

——A Clash of Kings

男人，真是一種不忠的生物！

——《烽火危城》下冊 p.249

Age makes ruin of us all.

——A Dance with Dragons

歲月不饒人。

——《與龍共舞》上冊 p.106

We are all going to die.

——A Dance with Dragons

人都會死。

——《與龍共舞》下冊 p.118

On Music

論音樂

Never believe anything you hear in a song.

　　　　　　　　　　　　　　——*A Storm of Swords*

不要相信妳聽到的歌詞。

　　　　　　　　　——《劍刃風暴》下冊 p.79

I have killed mothers, fathers, nephews, lovers, men and women, kings and whores. A singer once annoyed me, so I had the bastard stewed.

——*A Dance with Dragons*

我殺過的人，包括父親、母親、外甥和自己的愛人，上至君王，下至妓女，什麼樣的人都有。曾經有個唱歌的惹惱了我，隨後我就把他給煮了。

——《與龍共舞》中冊 p.157

If I am ever Hand again, the first thing I'll do is hang all the singers.

——*A Storm of Swords*

要是我再度當上御前首相，第一件要做的事就是把歌手全部絞死。

——《劍刃風暴》下冊 p.78

On Food and Drink

論美食與珍饌

I've heard the food in hell is wretched.

——*A Dance with Dragons*

聽說地獄的東西很噁心。

——《與龍共舞》中冊 p.46

I'm not fond of eating horse. Particularly *my* horse.

——*A Game of Thrones*

我本來就對吃馬肉沒興趣，尤其沒興趣吃自己的馬。

——《權力遊戲》上冊 p.433

Hors d'oeuvres 法文，意為冷盤。Hors(e) 則是馬。

Being randy is the next best thing to being drunk.

——*A Dance with Dragons*

醉後的好處多多，其一就是施展色心。

——《與龍共舞》上冊 p.254

Do I really want to spend the rest of my life eating salt beef and porridge with murderers and thieves?

——*A Dance with Dragons*

要我餘生陪著殺人犯和小偷一起吃粥配醃肉嗎？

——《與龍共舞》上冊 p.28

Someone should tell the cooks that turnip isn't a meat.

——*A Game of Thrones*

這些廚子到底知不知道蘿蔔和肉的差別？

——《權力遊戲》上冊 p.258

If I drink enough fire wine perhaps I'll dream of dragons.

——*A Dance with Dragons*

火酒若喝得夠多，也許就能夢見龍。

——《與龍共舞》上冊 p.107

On Kingship

論王者風範

All sorts of people are calling themselves kings these days.

——*A Clash of Kings*

這年頭什麼樣的人都能當國王。

——《烽火危城》上冊 p.66

My nephew is not fit to sit a privy, let alone the Iron Throne.

——A Clash of Kings

我那外甥連茅坑都不配坐，還談什麼鐵王座。

——《烽火危城》下冊 p.128

Crowns do queer things to the heads beneath them.

——A Clash of Kings

任誰戴了皇冠，腦筋都會不清楚。

——《烽火危城》上冊 p.75

Kings are falling like leaves this autumn.

——*A Storm of Swords*

今年秋天，國王像樹葉一樣落下。

——《劍刃風暴》中冊 p.432

On Realpolitik

論爭權奪利

Some allies are more dangerous than enemies.

——*A Dance with Dragons*

有些盟友比敵人更難對付。

——《與龍共舞》中冊 p.35

You can buy a man with gold, but only blood and steel will keep him true.

——*A Dance with Dragons*

金子當然可以收買人心，但要人心不變，還是得靠鮮血與鋼鐵。

——《與龍共舞》上冊 p.330

Schemes are like fruit, they require a certain ripening.

——*A Clash of Kings*

計謀就像水果，需要時間醞釀才會成熟。

——《烽火危城》上冊 p.79

It all goes back and back, to our mothers and fathers and theirs before them. We are puppets dancing on the strings of those who came before us, and one day our own children will take up our strings and dance in our steads.

——*A Storm of Swords*

這種事若往前追溯只會沒完沒了，追溯到我們的父母親，還有他們的父母親。我們都是被前人綁上線耍得團團轉的傀儡，而有朝一日我們的小孩也會接下這些線，代替我們團團轉。

——《劍刃風暴》下冊 p.247

Rebellion makes for queer bedfellows.

——A Dance with Dragons

為了造反，八竿子打不著的人都湊在一塊了。

——《與龍共舞》上冊 p.112

When winter comes, the realm will starve.

——*A Dance with Dragons*

到了冬天，全國都要挨餓。

——《與龍共舞》上冊 p.391

The Art of War

論戰爭之術

Gold has its uses, but wars are won with iron.

——*A Dance with Dragons*

錢的確有用，但戰爭還是得靠實力。

——《與龍共舞》上冊 p.114

I sit a chair better than a horse, and I'd sooner hold a wine goblet than a battle-axe. All that about the thunder of the drums, sunlight flashing on armor, magnificent destriers snorting and prancing? Well, the drums gave me headaches, the sunlight flashing on my armor cooked me up like a harvest day goose, and those magnificent destriers shit everywhere.

——*A Clash of Kings*

坐椅子總比騎馬要安穩多了，更何況我寧願拿酒杯，也不要拿戰斧。不是都說戰場上鼓聲雷動、金甲奪目、馬鳴蕭蕭嗎？哎，戰鼓敲得我頭疼，穿著盔甲都快被太陽烤熟了，簡直與豐收節慶上的烤鵝沒兩樣，至於那些駿馬，牠們就知道四處拉屎

——《烽火危城》上冊 p.70

How many Dornishmen does it take to start a war? Only one.

——*A Storm of Swords*

有多少冬恩人喜歡挑起紛爭？只有一個。

——《劍刃風暴》中冊 p.200

Knights know only one way to solve a problem. They couch their lances and charges. A dwarf has a different way of looking at the world.

——*A Dance with Dragons*

騎士解決問題的手段只有一種，就是提著長槍衝鋒。而侏儒看世界的角度本來就不一樣。

——《與龍共舞》上冊 p.109

He's going to be as useful as nipples on a breastplate.

——*A Dance with Dragons*

現在這個人就像胸甲上雕刻的乳頭一樣沒用。

——《與龍共舞》中冊 p.413

If a man paints a target on his chest, he should expect that sooner or later someone will loose an arrow at him.

——*A Game of Thrones*

如果有人在胸前畫靶，他就要有挨箭的心理準備。

——《權力遊戲》上冊 p.282

A sword through the bowels. A sure cure for constipation.

——A Dance with Dragons

舉劍直接插進肚子裡，剛好可以治便祕。

——《與龍共舞》中冊 p.47

Men fight more fiercely for a king who shares their peril than one who hides behind his mother's skirts.

——A Clash of Kings

國王若能與百姓有難同當，才能激勵士氣，不能老是躲在母親的裙後。

——《烽火危城》下冊 p.309

That was the way of war. The smallfolk were slaughtered, while highborn were held for ransom. *Remind me to thank the gods that I was born a Lannister.*

——*A Clash of Kings*

戰爭就是這樣！貴族被俘虜，等人來贖，平民就只有被屠殺的分。真要感謝諸神，讓我生在蘭尼斯特家。

——《烽火危城》上冊 p.359

The Art of Saving Your Skin

論自救之術

Courage and folly are cousins, or so I've heard.

——*A Clash of Kings*

我聽說勇氣和愚蠢往往只有一線之隔。

——《烽火危城》上冊 p.72

I'm terrified of my enemies, so I kill them all.

——*A Clash of Kings*

因為我很怕敵人，所以把他們通通殺光。

——《烽火危城》上冊 p.84

All this mistrust will sour your stomach and keep you awake at night, 'tis true, but better that than the long sleep that does not end.

——*A Dance with Dragons*

不信任別人，會害您半夜苦惱焦躁得睡不著，這我明白，問題是信錯了人，您就會一睡不醒。

——《與龍共舞》上冊 p.391

I decline to deliver any message that might get me killed.

——*A Game of Thrones*

我拒絕傳達可能會惹來殺身之禍的口信。

——《權力遊戲》上冊 p.292

（卷軸上的字）殺了傳信人

Riding hard and fast by night is a sure way to tumble down a mountain and crack your skull.

——*A Game of Thrones*

夜間趕路，本來就容易失足摔破腦袋。

——《權力遊戲》下冊 p.58

The Art of Lying

論說謊之術

Give me sweet lies, and keep your bitter truths.

——*A Storm of Swords*

給我甜言蜜語，殘酷的事實就請留著吧。

——《劍刃風暴》下冊 p.171

How did I lose my nose? I shoved it up your wife's cunt and she bit it off.

——*A Dance with Dragons*

你問我的鼻子怎麼不見了？我只是探頭到你老婆下面，鼻子就被她咬掉啦。

——《與龍共舞》中冊 p.419

Half-truths are worth more than outright lies.

——*A Storm of Swords*

真假參半，比起完全的謊言更厲害。

——《劍刃風暴》下冊 p.176

My father threw me down a well the day I was born, but I was so ugly that the water witch who lived down there spat me back.

——*A Dance with Dragons*

甫出生，我爸就把我丟進水井裡，可惜生得太醜，住在底下的水女巫又把我給噴了上來。

——《與龍共舞》上冊 p.258

The best lies are seasoned with a bit of truth.

——A Dance with Dragons

最高明的謊言，總是摻雜了真話。

——《與龍共舞》上冊 p.260

My mother loved me best of all her children because I was so small. She nursed me at her breast till I was seven. That made my brothers jealous, so they stuffed me in a sack and sold me to a mummer's troupe. When I tried to run off the master mummer cut off half my nose, so I had no choice but to go with them and learn to be amusing.

——*A Dance with Dragons*

因為個子小，幾個孩子裡，母親最疼愛我，直到七歲都還沒斷奶。哥哥們因為嫉妒，便拿布袋套了我，偷偷賣到劇團去。後來試圖想逃跑，結果被團長切下一半的鼻子，無奈只能跟他們走，然後想方設法逗人開心。

——《與龍共舞》上冊 p.258

The sow I ride is actually my sister. We have the same nose, could you tell? A wizard cast a spell on her, but if you give her a big wet kiss, she'll turn into a beautiful woman. The pity is, once you get to know her, you'll want to kiss her again to turn her back.

——*A Dance with Dragons*

其實我騎的那頭母豬是我妹，你應該看得出我們倆的鼻子長得一樣吧？她被個巫師下咒啦！
要是你願意伸舌頭好好吻她，她會變成一個漂亮的女人。
糟糕的是，等你和她相處後，就會想再親她一次，把她變回豬。

——《與龍共舞》下冊 p.126

Every touch a lie. I have paid her so much false coin that she half thinks she's rich.

——*A Dance with Dragons*

每次肢體接觸都是虛情假意！我給了她太多假錢，導致她覺得自己很有錢。

——《與龍共舞》下冊 p.131

You'd be astonished at what a boy can make of a few lies, fifty pieces of silver, and a drunken septon.

——A Game of Thrones

小男孩靠他幾句謊言、口袋的五十枚銀幣，還有一個醉酒的修士，很難不發生什麼大事！

——《權力遊戲》下冊 p.64

On Dragons
and Other Myths

論龍及其他神話

I believe in steel swords, gold coins, and men's wits. And I believe there once were dragons.

——*A Clash of Kings*

我相信刀劍、金錢和智慧，也相信世上曾經有龍。

——《烽火危城》下冊 p.176

What if we should find that this talk of dragons was just some sailor's drunken fancy? This wide world is full of such mad tales. Grumkins and snarks, ghosts and ghouls, mermaids, rock goblins, winged horses, winged pigs, winged lions.

——*A Dance with Dragons*

所謂的龍，其實都只是水手喝醉後的胡言亂語？這世上充斥著各種瘋狂傳聞，什麼魑魅魍魎、幽靈殭屍、人魚山怪、飛馬，甚至飛豬……飛獅之類。

——《與龍共舞》上冊 p.172

Next you will be offering me a suit of magic armor and a palace in Valyria.

——*A Dance with Dragons*

緊接著你是不是要給我一套魔法盔甲和瓦雷利亞的宮殿啊。

——《與龍共舞》上冊 p.103

Even a stunted, twisted, ugly little boy can look down over the world when he's seated on a dragon's back.

——A Game of Thrones

只要能騎在龍背上，即使是發育不良的畸形醜小孩，也可以睥睨全世界。

——《權力遊戲》上冊 p.175

Once a man has seen a dragon in flight, let him stay home and tend his garden in content, for this wide world has no greater wonder.

——*A Dance with Dragons*

只要看過翱翔天際的龍，就能心滿意足地回家種花，因為不會再有讓世人更想望的事情了。

——《與龍共舞》上冊 p.253

If you want to conquer the world, you best have dragons.

——A Dance with Dragons

想要征服世界，最好找到龍幫忙。

——《與龍共舞》上冊 p.263

The Shrouded Lord is just a legend, no more real than the ghost of Lann the Clever that some claim haunts Casterley Rock.

——*A Dance with Dragons*

籠霧王只是個傳說，就像有些人說機靈的蘭尼還陰魂不散的在凱岩城內，是同樣的意思。

——《與龍共舞》上冊 p.164

Trust no one. And keep your dragon close.

——*A Dance with Dragons*

誰都不要信。龍在身邊才有用。

——《與龍共舞》上冊 p.393

On Religion

論信仰

What sort of gods make rats and plagues and dwarfs?

——*A Dance with Dragons*

究竟怎樣的神，會創造出老鼠、瘟疫和侏儒呢？

——《與龍共舞》上冊 p.113

When I was a boy, my wet nurse told me that one day, if men were good, the gods would give the world a summer without ending.

——*A Game of Thrones*

小時候，奶媽告訴我，倘若有朝一日，人們都能和睦相處、知禮向善，那麼諸神便會讓盛夏永不消失。

——《權力遊戲》上冊 p.287

Light our fire and protect us from the dark, blah blah, light our way and keep us toasty warm, the night is dark and full of terrors, save us from the scary things, and blah blah blah some more.

——*A Dance with Dragons*

點亮火焰，保護我們不受黑暗玷汙……照亮前方，給予溫暖，即使長夜黑暗、處處險惡，也能保護我們不受可怕的東西侵擾。

——《與龍共舞》中冊 p.147

Somewhere some god is laughing.

——A Dance with Dragons

天上某處的某位神明正在看笑話吧！

——《與龍共舞》中冊 p.417

If there are gods to listen, they are monstrous gods, who torment us for their sport. Who else would make a world like this, so full of bondage, blood, and pain?

——*A Dance with Dragons*

倘若真有神明傾聽，也必然是性格扭曲的神才會折磨我們至此。否則為什麼會讓這世界充滿枷鎖、血腥及痛楚呢？

——《與龍共舞》下冊 p.130

The gods give with one hand and take with the other.

——*A Clash of Kings*

諸神一手給予、一手奪取。

——《烽火危城》下冊 p.243

If I could pray with my cock, I would be much more religious.

——*A Clash of Kings*

如果我可以用老二做禮拜，保證絕對虔誠。

——《烽火危城》上冊 p.273

（由上而下）與龍共舞，群鴉盛宴，劍刃風暴，烽火危城，權力遊戲

關於作者

　　喬治·R·R·馬丁是《紐約時報》多部暢銷小說的作者，包含受到高度讚揚的冰與火之歌系列——《權力遊戲》、《烽火危城》、《劍刃風暴》、《群鴉盛宴》、《與龍共舞》。身為一名作家兼製作人，他曾製作影集《陰陽魔界》、《美女與野獸》及多部史無前例的電影和首播影集。與太太芭莉絲住在新墨西哥的聖塔菲。

www.georgerrmartin.com

高寶書版集團
gobooks.com.tw

FN 066
冰與火之歌之小惡魔的大智慧
The Wit & Wisdom of Tyrion Lannister

作　　者　喬治・馬汀（George R. R. Martin）
繪　　圖　強堤・克拉克（Jonty Clark）
整理／翻譯　林零
編　　輯　林俶萍
校　　對　李思佳・林俶萍
排　　版　趙小芳
美術編輯　林政嘉
企　　畫　林佩蓉

2017.9.18

發 行 人　朱凱蕾
出　　版　英屬維京群島商高寶國際有限公司台灣分公司
　　　　　Global Group Holdings, Ltd.
地　　址　台北市內湖區洲子街88號3樓
網　　址　gobooks.com.tw
電　　話　(02) 27992788
電　　郵　readers@gobooks.com.tw（讀者服務部）
　　　　　pr@gobooks.com.tw（公關諮詢部）
傳　　真　出版部　(02) 27990909　行銷部 (02) 27993088
郵政劃撥　19394552
戶　　名　英屬維京群島商高寶國際有限公司台灣分公司
發　　行　希代多媒體書版股份有限公司/Printed in Taiwan
初版日期　2015年2月
The Wit & Wisdom of Tyrion Lannister
Copyright ©2013 by George R.R. Martin
This edition arranged with The Lotts Agency Ltd.
trough Andrew Nurnberg Associates International Limited
Cover illustration by Jonty Clark
Cover design layout © HarperCollinsPublishers Ltd 2013

國家圖書館出版品預行編目(CIP)資料

冰與火之歌之小惡魔的大智慧 ／ 喬治・馬汀
（George R. R. Martin）著，強堤・克拉克
（Jonty Clark）繪圖，林零整理／翻譯. -- 初版. --
臺北市：高寶國際出版：希代多媒體發行, 2015.02
　面；　公分. -- (奇幻文學；FN 066)
譯自：The Wit & Wisdom of Tyrion Lannister
ISBN 978-986-185-887-6(平裝)

874.6　　　　　　　　　　　104001277